DANCING TURTLE

Adapted from an American Folk Tale

By Maggie Duff

Illustrated by Maria Horvath

Macmillan Publishing Co., Inc. / New York

Collier Macmillan Publishers / London

Dancing Turtle is adapted from a story in *Louisiana Folk Tales,*
from the Alice Fortier Memoirs, Volume II, 1895.

Macmillan Publishing Co., Inc.
866 Third Avenue, New York, N.Y. 10022
Collier Macmillan Canada, Ltd.
Printed in the United States of America

10 9 8 7 6 5 4 3 2 1

LIBRARY OF CONGRESS CATALOGING IN PUBLICATION DATA
Duff, Maggie.   Dancing Turtle.
   Adaptation of Tortoise, from Louisiana folk-tales,
collected and edited by A. Fortier, 1895.
   SUMMARY: Lured into captivity when her singing is
praised, a many-talented turtle charms her hungry
captors and dances to freedom.
   [1. Folklore—United States] I. Horvath, Maria,
date. II. Tortie. English. III. Title.
PZ8.1.D84Dan 1981   398.2′ 452792′ 0973 [E]
ISBN 0-02-733010-9   80-24683

To Brady

— M. D.

To my sister Irén

—M. H.

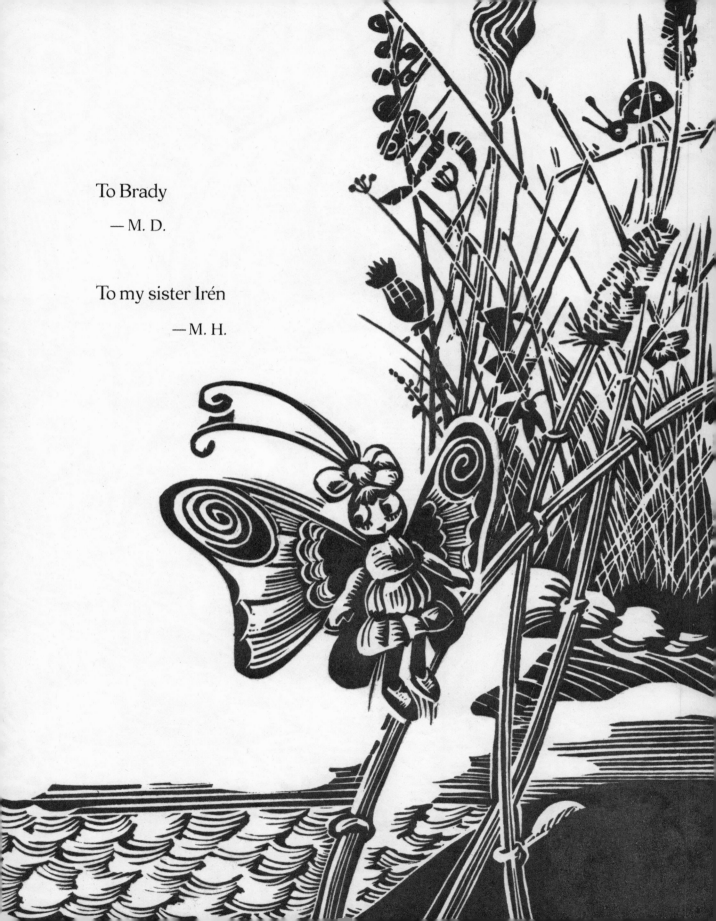

Once, not so very long ago, three good
friends lived together near a bayou. Now,
a bayou is a wet and marshy kind of place,
with streams running through it like
ribbons, and Jake and Willie and Tom often
fished in these streams for their supper.

One warm and sunny day, Jake decided to get an early start, so he set off by himself for his usual fishing spot. Soon he came to his favorite rock, tied up his raft, put out his pole, and sat quietly dreaming of the fine mess of fish he'd bring back. Suddenly, he heard a soft and silvery sound.

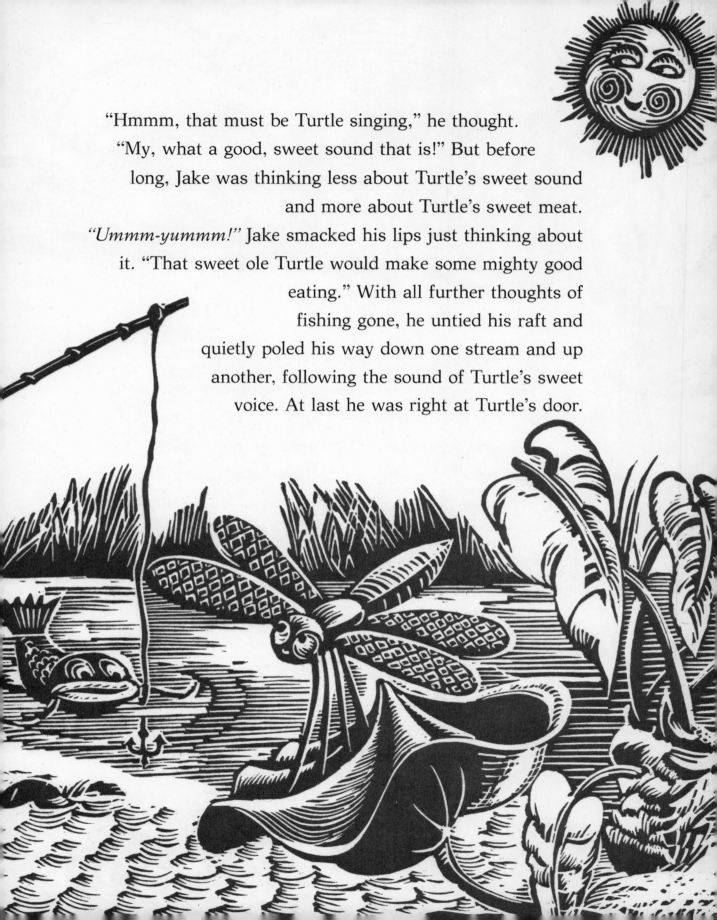

"Hmmm, that must be Turtle singing," he thought. "My, what a good, sweet sound that is!" But before long, Jake was thinking less about Turtle's sweet sound and more about Turtle's sweet meat. *"Ummm-yummm!"* Jake smacked his lips just thinking about it. "That sweet ole Turtle would make some mighty good eating." With all further thoughts of fishing gone, he untied his raft and quietly poled his way down one stream and up another, following the sound of Turtle's sweet voice. At last he was right at Turtle's door.

Jake knocked and called out, "Ho, Turtle!
That is mighty fine singing. Come on out
so I can hear you better."
The singing stopped, but Turtle did not come to
the door. Then, after a bit, the singing continued.
This time Jake knocked twice and called out loudly,
"Ho, Turtle, I say! That is *mighty* fine singing.
I certainly do like it. Won't you *please*
come out so I can hear you better?"
Again the singing stopped, but this time,
c-r-u-n-chh...c-r-u-n-chh...c-r-u-n-chh...,
Turtle came slowly to the door. "Do you really
like my singing?" she asked, peering out cautiously.
"Oh, yes. I surely do. Please come out so
I can hear you better," coaxed Jake.

Turtle was pleased. She opened the
door and, *crunch…crunch…crunch…*, she
moved outside. Quick as a flash, Jake
grabbed her by the tail.
"Aha! Fooled you, Turtle," he laughed.
"Now it's home for supper!"

Carefully, Jake turned Turtle upside down, tied a rope
to her tail, and headed for his raft. Poor Turtle!
She could only try to see where she was being taken
and hope for the best.

When Jake reached home, Tom and Willie were waiting for him.
"What's for dinner, Jake?" they asked. "Did you
catch anything?"
"Sure did—caught a fine ole sweet-singing
turtle," Jake sang out.

"Turtle! What'll we do with a
turtle?" moaned Tom and Willie.
"We'll make a fine turtle stew, that's
what we'll do," Jake shouted happily.
"And since this is such a big ole
turtle, we'll have enough stew to have us a party! Now
come on and help me build a cage to keep this sweet turtle
safe while I go fetch our friends." When Turtle heard this,
she was so frightened she pulled herself into her shell.
As soon as they heard the word "party," Willie and Tom
stopped grumbling and quickly began gathering pieces of
wood for the cage. When they had enough, Willie pounded the
stakes into the ground, then wound a rope back and forth
and in between to make a proper cage.
Then Jake picked up Turtle, placed her inside, and hopped
back on his raft.
"Now remember," he called out as he shoved away from the
bank, "keep your eye on Turtle. Don't let her out of the
cage, or we'll lose our supper for sure!"
After Jake had gone, Tom and Willie sat quietly, looking
at Turtle, hoping she would come out of her shell.
But she didn't, and they soon grew tired of waiting and
set off to gather fruit and nuts for the party.

When all was still, Turtle came slowly out of her shell.
First she poked out her head. Next came her feet and legs.
Last of all came her tail. Blinking her eyes, she looked
around the cage and crawled over to one side to think.
She sat there remembering what Jake had said about supper.
And she knew she had to find a way to escape.
Soon Turtle began singing. She sang high
notes and she sang low
notes, and she always
sang sweet notes.

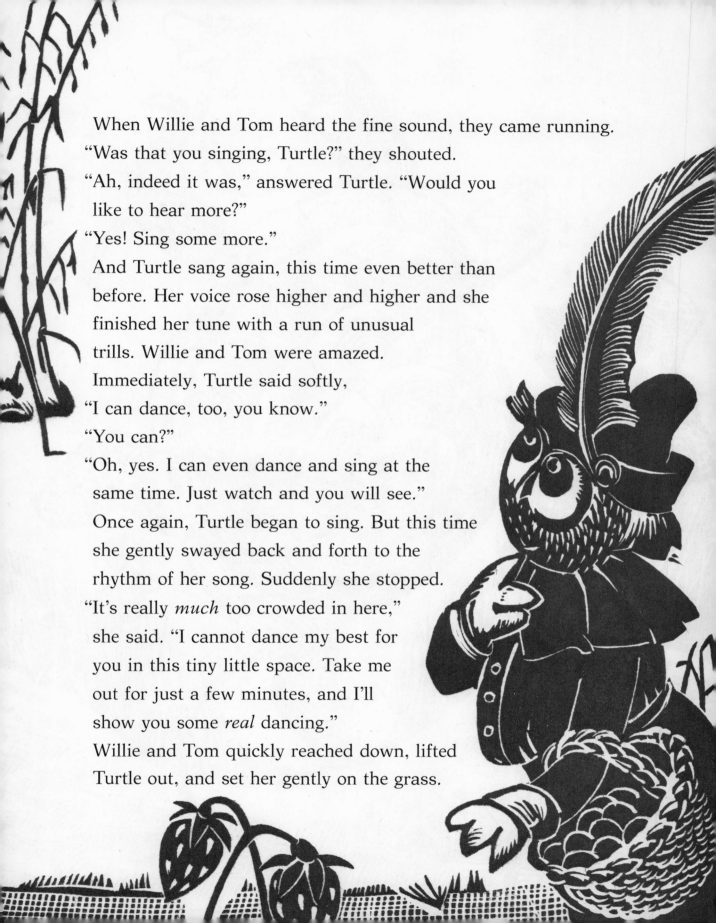

When Willie and Tom heard the fine sound, they came running.
"Was that you singing, Turtle?" they shouted.
"Ah, indeed it was," answered Turtle. "Would you
like to hear more?"
"Yes! Sing some more."
And Turtle sang again, this time even better than
before. Her voice rose higher and higher and she
finished her tune with a run of unusual
trills. Willie and Tom were amazed.
Immediately, Turtle said softly,
"I can dance, too, you know."
"You can?"
"Oh, yes. I can even dance and sing at the
same time. Just watch and you will see."
Once again, Turtle began to sing. But this time
she gently swayed back and forth to the
rhythm of her song. Suddenly she stopped.
"It's really *much* too crowded in here,"
she said. "I cannot dance my best for
you in this tiny little space. Take me
out for just a few minutes, and I'll
show you some *real* dancing."
Willie and Tom quickly reached down, lifted
Turtle out, and set her gently on the grass.

"Ah, much better," said Turtle, nibbling a few blades of grass and stretching this way and that. Then she stood on her back legs and began to sing very softly. And as she sang, she began to dance. She dipped to the left and spun to the right, and her voice grew sweeter with each step. Then, after dancing right to the edge of the stream, Turtle disappeared with a splash!

When Tom and Willie realized what had happened, they went
running up and down the banks of the stream, calling and
looking for Turtle. "Come back, Turtle. Come back!" they
cried. But, of course, Turtle did not come back.
And then Tom remembered what Jake had said.
"Yo ho! Jake will be mad when he comes back and finds
Turtle gone," wailed Tom. "What shall we do?"
"Well, we'll just have to think of something, that's what,"
said Willie. And the two friends paced back and forth,
back and forth, until they had a plan.
First they found a stone the same size and shape as
Turtle. Then they painted it to look just like Turtle
and placed it in the cage, just so.

"Jake will never know the difference!" said Tom hopefully.
"He'll be fooled for sure," agreed Willie. As they talked,
Jake returned with their friends.

"Time to eat!" he shouted happily. "Let's get that
sweet-singing ole Turtle to cooking. Tom,
Willie—bring over a pot of water while I get
the fire going."

Without a word, Tom and Willie filled the pot and
brought it to the fire. When the water was boiling
fiercely, Jake picked up what he thought to be
Turtle and dropped it into the water.

Everyone—except Tom and Willie—laughed and joked
and talked about the wonderful meal they were
about to have.

When the cooking time was up, Jake called for Turtle to be brought to the table. The guests gathered around expectantly as Jake began to carve. But the knife bounced off the stone!

"What's this?" demanded Jake. "Now don't tell me my
sweet-singing Turtle is just a tough ole bird after all.
Well, we'll soon see about that!"

Jake left the table and came back carrying his ax.
Tom and Willie remained silent while everyone else
laughed and teased Jake. But Jake paid no attention.
He raised the ax high over his head
and brought it down with a great thunk!

Jake picked up Tom and Willie's turtle and looked at it closely. "Hmmm," he muttered. "Are these ole eyes fooling me, or is this a rock?" He looked at Tom and then he looked at Willie. "How did this happen?" he asked. Neither Tom nor Willie said a word.
"Did you let that sweet-singing Turtle out of her cage?" growled Jake.

Finally, Willie spoke. "It was because of Turtle's dancing. Did you know she could *dance?* She could even dance and sing at the same time! But then she danced into the water—right out of sight. Oh, Jake, we didn't mean to let her go. Please don't get mad."

Now Jake was silent. Then, after a bit, he said, "A dancing turtle, eh? Danced right out of sight, you say? Now there's a sight I'd like to see!" And he started to laugh. And he laughed until tears rolled down his cheeks. Then everyone began to laugh.

"Ho!" said Jake, catching his breath. "There's not much left in the way of a supper, but there's nothing to stop us from having a good time. C'mon, everyone. Let's dance!"

And the moon came up and the stars glistened as the friends laughed and danced the night away.

And, for all we know, they all could still be laughing
and dancing somewhere deep in that old bayou.
And Turtle must surely still be sweetly singing.